Dear Parents and Educators,

Welcome to Penguin Young Readers! As parents and educators, you know that each child develops at his or her own pace—in terms of speech, critical thinking, and, of course, reading. Penguin Young Readers recognizes this fact. As a result, each Penguin Young Readers book is assigned a traditional easy-to-read level (1–4) as well as a Guided Reading Level (A–P). Both of these systems will help you choose the right book for your child. Please refer to the back of each book for specific leveling information. Penguin Young Readers features esteemed authors and illustrators, stories about favorite characters, fascinating nonfiction, and more!

Max Finds an Egg

LEVEL **1**

GUIDED
READING
LEVEL **C**

This book is perfect for an **Emergent Reader** who:
- can read in a left-to-right and top-to-bottom progression;
- can recognize some beginning and ending letter sounds;
- can use picture clues to help tell the story; and
- can understand the basic plot and sequence of simple stories.

Here are some **activities** you can do during and after reading this book:
- Character Traits: In this story, we learn about Max and what he likes to do with his pets. Come up with a list of words that describe Max.
- Read the Pictures: Use the pictures to tell the story. Have the child go through the book, retelling the story just by looking at the pictures.

Remember, sharing the love of reading with a child is the best gift you can give!

—Bonnie Bader, EdM
 Penguin Young Readers program

*Penguin Young Readers are leveled by independent reviewers applying the standards developed by Irene Fountas and Gay Su Pinnell in *Matching Books to Readers: Using Leveled Books in Guided Reading*, Heinemann, 1999.

Dedicated to Ben-Ben and many fun
discoveries together—WB

For Erin—BC

PENGUIN YOUNG READERS
Published by the Penguin Group
Penguin Group (USA) LLC, 375 Hudson Street, New York, New York 10014, USA

USA | Canada | UK | Ireland | Australia | New Zealand | India | South Africa | China

penguin.com
A Penguin Random House Company

Library of Congress Cataloging-in-Publication Data is available.

ISBN 978-0-448-47993-4 (pbk)   10 9 8 7 6 5
ISBN 978-0-448-47994-1 (hc)   10 9 8 7 6 5 4 3 2 1

Max Finds an Egg

by Wiley Blevins
illustrated by Ben Clanton

Penguin Young Readers
An Imprint of Penguin Group (USA) LLC

Max finds an egg.

It is big.

Is it a dinosaur egg?

Every boy wants a dinosaur.

So Max makes a nest.

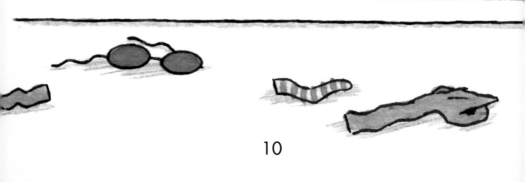

He puts a light on the egg.

13

He dances around the egg.

He waits.

And he waits.

Then peck, peck, peck.

CRACK!

Out pops a chicken.

Max cannot ride a chicken.

But the chicken likes to run.

And hide.

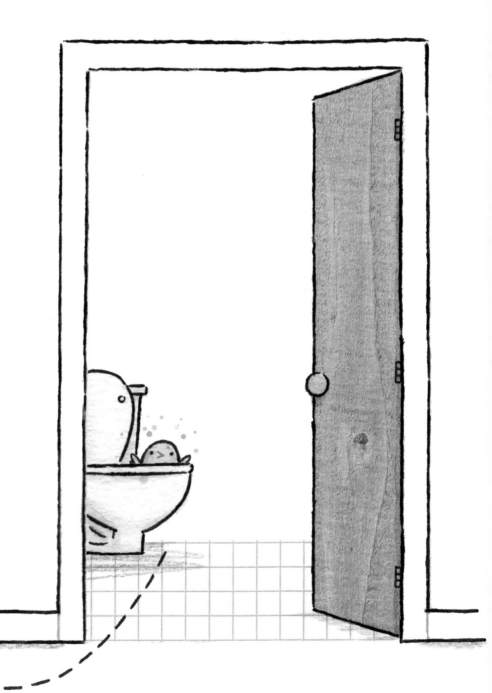

And dance with Max.

Dance. Dance. Dance!